Hush, Little Baby

MARGOT ZEMACH

Hush, Little Baby

E. P. Dutton   New York

Illustrations copyright © 1976 by Margot Zemach
All rights reserved.

Unicorn is a registered trademark of E. P. Dutton.

Library of Congress number 76-5477

ISBN 0-525-44297-9

Published in the United States by E. P. Dutton,
2 Park Avenue, New York, N.Y. 10016

Published simultaneously in Canada by
Fitzhenry & Whiteside Limited, Toronto

Book design and title hand-lettering by Riki Levinson

Printed in Hong Kong by South China Printing Co.
First Unicorn Edition 1987   COBE
10 9 8 7 6 5 4 3 2 1

For Auntie Rees of Crooms Hill Grove, London,
with our love

Hush, little baby,
Don't say a word,

Poppa's gonna buy you
a mockingbird.
If that mockingbird won't sing,

Poppa's gonna buy you
  a diamond ring.
If that diamond ring turns brass,

Poppa's gonna buy you
a looking glass.
If that looking glass gets broke,

Poppa's gonna buy you
a billy goat.
If that billy goat won't pull,

Poppa's gonna buy you
a cart and bull.
If that cart and bull turn over,

Poppa's gonna buy you
a dog named Rover.

If that dog named Rover won't bark,

Poppa's gonna buy you
a horse and cart.

If that horse and cart

fall down,

You'll still be the sweetest
baby in town.

Hush, Little Baby

Hush, lit - tle ba - by, don't say a word,

Pop-pa's gon-na buy you a mock-ing-bird.

If that mock-ing - bird won't sing,

Pop-pa's gon-na buy you a dia-mond ring.

If that diamond ring turns brass,
Poppa's gonna buy you a looking glass.
If that looking glass gets broke,
Poppa's gonna buy you a billy goat.

If that billy goat won't pull,
Poppa's gonna buy you a cart and bull.
If that cart and bull turn over,
Poppa's gonna buy you a dog named Rover.

If that dog named Rover won't bark,
Poppa's gonna buy you a horse and cart.
If that horse and cart fall down,
You'll still be the sweetest baby in town.

MARGOT ZEMACH is the distinguished illustrator of many books, including *Mommy, Buy Me a China Doll; The Judge;* and *Duffy and the Devil,* winner of the Caldecott Medal (all published by Farrar, Straus & Giroux).

She says that she began to consider *Hush, Little Baby* a "tried and true" lullaby after singing it to her daughter Rebecca every night for a year and a half. During that time, the pictures of a large, untidy Mum; downtrodden, anxious Dad; and squalling baby seemed to form themselves in her mind—undoubtedly with a British flavor due to the fact that she was then living in London.

The artist now lives in Berkeley, California.